God Is with Me through the Day

written by Julie Cantrell

ZONDER**kidz**

ZONDERVAN.com/
AUTHOR**TRACKER**
follow your favorite authors

God Is with Me Through the Day
Copyright © 2009 by Julie Cantrell

Requests for information should be addressed to:
Zonderkidz, Grand Rapids, Michigan 49530

Library of Congress Cataloging-in-Publication Data

Cantrell, Julie, 1973-
     God is with me through the day / by Julie Cantrell.
         p. cm.
     Summary: A child is reminded that God loves him all the time, even when he
is alone.
     ISBN-13: 978-0-310-71562-7 (hardcover)
     ISBN-10: 0-310-71562-8 (hardcover)
     [1. Christian life--Fiction. 2. Fear--Fiction.] I. Title.
   PZ7.C173566Gl 2009
   [E]--dc22
   {B}   2007022904

Published in association with the literary agency of WordServe Literary Group, LTD., 10152 S. Knoll Circle, Highlands Ranch, Colorado 80130

Zonderkidz is a trademark of Zondervan.

Design: Jody Langley

Photo Credits:
Page 20: Thorsten Milse/Robert Harding World Imagery/Getty Images
Page 24: ©John W. Herbst/Corbis
Page 25: Martin Harvey/Gallo Images/Getty Images
Page 28: Wayne R Bilenduke/Stone/Getty Images

Printed in China

09 10 11 12 13 • 5 4 3 2 1

to Emily and Adam

In the morning

I wake up and stretch.

I play.

I am happy with my family.

I am **safe** in my **home.**

Then Mama kisses
my cheek.

And
I run
out
the
door.

I start to feel alone.

I try to be **brave.**

But
sometimes
I cry

I feel very small in the great big world.

That's when I remember that
God is **always** with me.

Just like when he helped David fight the lions to save his sheep.

Just like when God kept Jonah safe inside the whale.

I roar like a bear,
"I am safe!"

My world doesn't seem so scary anymore.

In God's
hands,
I am
strong.

I am loved!

And I am **never**

alone.

"When I am afraid, I will trust in you."

—Psalm 56:3

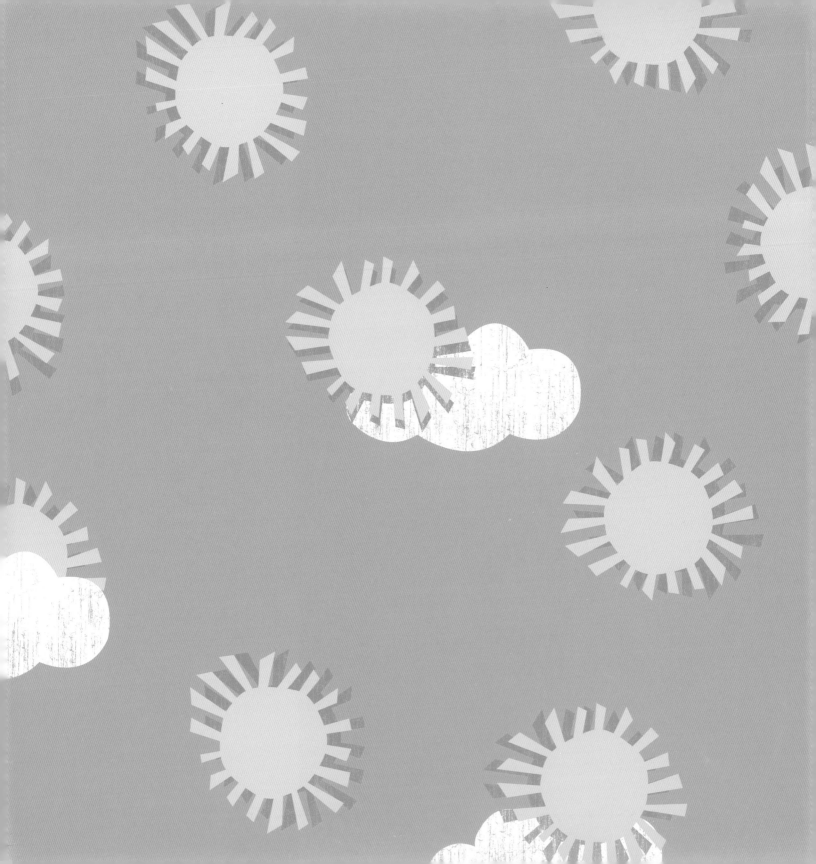